White Wolves Series Consultant: Sue Ellis,
Centre for Literacy in Primary Education

This book can be used in the White Wolves Guided Reading programme
to help less confident readers in Year 5 gain more independence

Reprinted 2011
First published 2009 by
A & C Black Publishers Ltd
36 Soho Square, London, W1D 3QY

www.acblack.com

Text copyright © 2009 Patrice Lawrence
Illustrations copyright © 2009 Adam Larkum

The rights of Patrice Lawrence and Adam Larkum
to be identified as the author and illustrator of this work
respectively have been asserted by them in accordance
with the Copyrights, Designs and Patents Act 1988.

ISBN 978-1-4081-1156-7

A CIP catalogue for this book is available from the British Library.

This book is produced using paper that is made from wood grown
in managed, sustainable forests. It is natural, renewable and
recyclable. The logging and manufacturing processes conform
to the environmental regulations of the country of origin.

Printed and bound in Great Britain
by CPI Cox & Wyman, Reading, RG1 8EX

WHITE WOLVES

GRANNY TING TING

Patrice Lawrence

Illustrated by Adam Larkum

A & C Black • London

GRANNY TING TING

Contents

Chapter One

It was a warm Caribbean evening. Ten-year-old Shayla was sitting on Granny's porch, kicking her feet impatiently.

"How much longer now?" she asked.

"They've only just left the airport," Mommy said. "Why don't you go

inside and keep Granny company?"

Granny had recently had an eye operation. Now she could almost see properly, but still found things difficult.

Shayla's cousin Michael and Aunty Jess were coming to Arouca to help Granny get better.

Michael was born in Trinidad, like Shayla, but moved to London when he was a baby. On his last visit, four years ago, the cousins had great fun chasing Granny's chickens and playing hide-and-seek in the bamboo by the river.

Shayla couldn't wait to see Michael again. She jumped up from her seat and ran to the gate as a car crawled slowly towards the house.

"Is that them?" she cried.

But the car carried on.

Shayla sat down again. She was too excited to read, so she watched the fireflies' shining green bottoms bump together under the papaya tree.

Deep in the bushes, the cicadas screeched their night song.

"Queetch, queek, queel," Shayla repeated. "You're so noisy!"

"They're calling for girlfriends," Mommy said. "They have flaps on their tummy. They pull them in and out to make all that noise."

Shayla took a deep breath and

pulled her tummy in tight. She let out the breath and her tummy relaxed.

In, out, in, out, very quickly. But all Shayla could manage was a strange, puffy noise and a squeal.

Mommy laughed.

"I think you need flaps to make it work."

Another car was approaching. Its headlights were bright against the dark road.

"Look!" Mommy said. "This could be them!"

Shayla ran back to the gate.

The car was going to turn the corner.

It slowed down. And stopped.

"Go on," Mommy urged. "This is
the moment you've been waiting for."

But Shayla suddenly felt shy.

Mommy rushed out of the house
towards the visitors. Granny followed
slowly behind her.

Aunty Jess climbed out of the car.
She had thin, twisted dreadlocks tied
back with a silver scarf.

Granny and Aunty Jess had a long

hug. Then Mommy and Aunty Jess
had a long hug.

Shayla wondered if she should go
and take part in some long hugging,
too. But she stayed where she was,
staring at the car. Was that shadowy

figure Michael? Why didn't he get out and say hello?

"Shayla's so excited," Mommy was saying. "She's been bouncing around like a grasshopper all week."

Great. Now Michael would think she was really stupid. Shayla marched towards the car, and was instantly scooped up into Aunty Jess's arms.

"Oh, my little darling!" Aunty Jess planted a kiss on Shayla's forehead. Shayla buried her face in Aunty's jacket, hoping to smell England.

Aunty Jess held Shayla's shoulders and stared at her. "You have grown so much!"

Shayla noticed a golden stud in Aunty's eyebrow and wondered if Granny would approve of that!

"And what about my Michael?" Aunty Jess pointed to the figure who was now standing by the car. There was a hint of mischief in her voice. "Has he grown, too?"

Shayla glanced across. Michael seemed much taller than before and

looked very grown-up and fashionable.

He was wearing baggy jeans, a white

T-shirt and a baseball cap pulled low

over his forehead.

The boy gave a tired smile and stared at the ground.

"Don't worry about him," Aunty Jess said. "He's going through his grumpy phase. And if he's anything like his dad, that's not likely to end soon."

Mommy and Aunty Jess laughed.

Michael did not.

"Don't upset the boy." Granny steered everyone into the house. "It's been such a long time since our family was together."

Then she pulled the sliding door shut against the night.

Chapter Two

Next morning, Shayla woke to the

sound of the radio and the clatter of

cooking pans. Comforting home noises.

Though this wasn't Shayla's home.

Her house was half an hour's drive

away. But she and Mommy had been

staying with Granny ever since the

eye operation.

Daddy didn't mind because he was away in America for a month, teaching in a university.

Granny's house was built on brick and concrete "stilts". Under the house, they kept a large freezer, empty bottles to return to the shops and Grandpa's old, rusting bike. Beyond was Granny's back yard, which was bursting with fruit trees and Shayla's very own vegetable patch.

Shayla stood outside Michael's room for a few minutes, but there was

no sound. She went into the kitchen.
Mommy was squeezing limes to make
juice. The skins were heaped in a pile
by the sink.

"Can I wake Michael up?"

"He's having a good sleep so
his body can set to Trinidad time."
Mommy squeezed the last lime and
washed her hands. "But later on, you
can both help Granny make tamarind
balls. Is that OK?"

Shayla nodded. She grabbed a
yogurt from the fridge and went to sit

on the steps overlooking the back
yard. Three years ago, Mommy had
planted a powderpuff tree. Now, a
jewel-coloured hummingbird darted
around the fluffy, pink blossoms.

The neighbour's mango tree was full of green fruit. Shayla hoped some ripe ones would fall on Granny's side.

And then there was Shayla's favourite lime tree. She loved climbing high into its branches and watching the world below.

Michael woke up at midday. He still looked tired and grumpy, and rather hot in his hooded sweatshirt and jeans.

The cousins stared at each other, then Michael grinned. "I've brought

you a present." He rummaged in his

pockets. "It's a pet."

It must be small, thought Shayla.

A mouse, or maybe a beetle. How did

he stop it escaping on the plane?

"Here." Michael handed her a

small box. "All the girls have them

in London."

Shayla opened the box, emptied

it out and peered into its corners.

"Did it run away?"

"No!"

On the table was something round

and purple. It had a screen and five
buttons set in the shape of a paw print.

"Is this the pet?"

"Yes," Michael said. "You have
to give it a name. Then you use those
buttons to feed it and take it for a
walk."

The thing beeped at Shayla.
She put it down on the table.

"Thank you," she said.

"Shayla!" Mommy was calling.
She and Aunty Jess came in from the
porch. "I'm taking Jess over to our

house. She's promised to help me tackle that wild garden of ours. And I need to pick up some more clothes for you."

Aunty Jess smiled. "I'm not sure about the gardening. But I wouldn't mind catching up on some gossip!"

"Can me and Michael come?" asked Shayla.

"I thought you were going to help Granny make tamarind balls," Mommy said.

Shayla could see Granny through the glass door leading to the porch.

She was lying back in a chair with her eyes closed. The day was hot, but Granny wore a thick sweater. She didn't look like the same Granny who had chased a big lizard from under the house last year.

Michael was frowning.

"Don't worry," Aunty Jess chuckled. "We'll be back in a couple of hours, and Shayla will look after you."

Mommy and Aunty Jess left.

Michael stomped around the back yard frightening the chickens and kicking up clouds of dust.

"What's the matter?" Shayla asked.

"I'm older than you. I don't need looking after."

"But you don't know where things are!"

"Wanna bet?"

Michael clomped down beneath the house. Shayla followed him.

"Michael? What are you...? No! You're not allowed!"

But it was too late. Michael had pulled out the rusty old bicycle and was wheeling it towards the road.

"Granny!" Shayla yelled. "Michael's going!"

Granny came onto the porch. With a *ting* of the bell, Michael was gone.

"He'll get lost!" Shayla peered

down the road. "Shall I call the police?"

Granny shook her head. "He'll be back soon. Anyway, it's nice to see that old bicycle on the road again."

"Did you ever ride it?"

"No, darling. I tried so many times. I just couldn't work it out. But when your grandpa died, I knew I could never give it away."

"Because it reminds you of him?" Shayla loved it when Granny told her stories about the past.

"Well," Granny said, with a slightly sad smile. "When Grandpa and I got married, nobody we knew owned a car. And I refused to leave church in a horse and cart!

"So Grandpa tied a huge, yellow bow to the handlebars of that bike, and I sat side-saddle on the crossbar. He pedalled me two miles down the road to our new home."

"Did he have to go up any hills?"

"Just a small one. But there were lots of potholes! There still are, and

31

maybe they got the better of your

cousin. Look! Here he comes now."

With a clank and squeal, Michael

stopped outside the houe. His face was

covered with sweat.

"It's easy to find your way round

if you're used to London."

He gave a slightly embarrassed smile and wiped his wet forehead with his sleeve. "Of course, I could have gone further, but I didn't want to worry you."

Chapter Three

Shayla loved the way tamarind balls filled your mouth with sweetness and sourness at the same time. The brown, sugary sweets were definitely one of her favourites.

"Do you have tamarind balls in England?" she asked.

"Yes," Michael said. "In London

you can get anything. Our market sells sweets from Trinidad and India and Nigeria... Everywhere!"

"Well," Shayla said. "I'm sure the tamarind balls in London aren't nearly as tasty as Granny's."

Granny let Michael split open the brown tamarind pods and scrape the pulp into a bowl. That was usually Shayla's job. She stood by the fridge watching him.

"I bet people from London can't eat tamarinds as they are," she said.

Michael looked at her.

"Shayla..." Granny warned.

But Michael spooned up some pulp and shoved it into his mouth. His eyes widened as the sourness pinched his tongue.

Shayla grinned. "Can you hold it in there for a minute?"

Michael closed his eyes.

Shayla looked at the clock.

"Time's up! Now how about some ginger beer to wash it down?"

"Don't make mischief, Shayla," Granny said. "That will be too spicy for Michael."

But her grandson was already at the fridge door. He found the jug of ginger beer, poured a glass and took a massive gulp.

"Aaagh!" Michael snorted and his eyes watered.

Shayla went over and poured a glass for herself. She sipped and closed her eyes in enjoyment.

"I bet ginger beer's not this hot in London."

Michael glared at her.

"Of course it is! And I can eat much hotter things than that! Granny, what's the spiciest thing in your fridge?"

"Granny's hot, hot, hot pepper sauce," Shayla replied. "Even my uncles only have a tiny bit of that."

Michael rummaged in the fridge. He held up a jar of fiery red-and-yellow mush.

"I think you should leave that alone," Granny said firmly.

But Michael wrenched off the lid and plunged his finger into the sauce. Shayla sneezed as the hot pepper fumes wafted up her nose. Michael breathed in and stuck his finger in his mouth.

Silence.

Shock.

A hundred soldier ants were biting his tongue.

It was the hottest thing in the whole world and it was stuck to the inside of Michael's mouth.

Michael gasped. His eyes streamed. His nose dripped. His throat opened and closed and a strange gargling sound came out.

"Ice," Granny ordered. "Quick!"

Shayla ran down to the freezer under the house, tripping over the old bike in her hurry. She grabbed a

handful of ice cubes and rushed back to Michael. He sucked one slowly.

"My!" Granny looked at Michael with amusement. "You're a bold one."

"Your turn," Michael said, offering the jar to Shayla.

But Shayla shook her head.

"In Trinidad, we are much more sensible."

It was late afternoon. Granny had given Michael two bowls of homemade ice cream to help take away the taste

of the pepper. Now she was showing

him around the back yard. Shayla

trailed behind.

"That's cocoa." Granny pointed

to a small tree with big, orangey pods

hanging from its trunk and branches.

"You can see sugar cane at the back.

That cashew is new since you were last

here. And over there? That's stinking

toe." She showed him a big tree with

fat, brown, knobbly pods. It looked like

a small giant was dangling his feet

through the branches.

"What's the stinking bit about?" Michael asked.

"When the fruit's ripe…" Granny held her nose. "Imagine the stinkiest sneakers left out in the rain overnight."

"Yuk," said Shayla and Michael together.

"And this…" Granny stood by a tall, thick-trunked tree. "Is our lime. It takes up so much space, we want to cut it down, but Shayla won't let us."

"It's my climbing tree," Shayla said. "London doesn't have any trees,

does it? Only high buildings and cars."

"Of course there are trees in London," Michael said. "And I bet I can climb higher than you."

"Go on, then!"

"Oh, you children!" Granny shrugged and went back inside.

Michael grasped the trunk and found his first foothold. He heaved himself up and pulled himself onto the lower branches. Then higher and higher. He poked his head through the top leaves and waved.

"Your turn," Michael said, scrambling down.

No problem. Shayla gripped the trunk and pulled herself up. This was *her* tree. She knew every branch. Every twig. She had done this hundreds of times. Nothing was going to stop her showing Michael how…

And then she saw it.

A fat, black-and-yellow striped body. Orange, spotty feet. A bright-red head.

It was crawling towards her.

Just a caterpillar. Harmless. But…

"Aaaagghhhhhh!"

Shayla came down much quicker than she'd gone up, crashing through the branches, leaping onto the dusty ground. She picked herself up and brushed some chicken poo from her T-shirt.

"I think I won that contest, too," Michael laughed. "There's an adventure playground near my home in London. The climbing frame's much harder to get up than this tree!"

Chapter Four

Night comes quickly in Trinidad, like someone's kicked the sun to the other side of the world and dropped the moon into its place.

Aunty Jess and Mommy were washing up. The television was on. A man lay bound in bandages like a mummy, trying to speak. Granny

loved soap operas. She knew all the characters just from their voices.

"Tell them where you hid the money," Granny said loudly.

Shayla was used to Granny talking to the television, but Michael looked alarmed.

The bandaged man opened his eyes. Moved his lips. Then…

Darkness. Silence.

Shayla's heart thumped.

A mosquito buzzed near her ear.

She could hear Michael breathing.

"It's just a power cut," Granny said. "There are plenty of candles."

Mommy rattled around in the kitchen drawers and soon the room filled with flickering light.

Aunty Jess giggled. "This used to happen all the time when we were little."

Mommy agreed. "And those stories Granny would tell us. They were terrifying! Especially the one about Uncle William. I'll never forget that."

"What happened?" Shayla asked.

"I'm no good at telling stories," said Mommy.

"Can you tell it, Granny?" asked Michael.

"Well…" Granny said. "Uncle William was coming home late one night, when he heard a baby crying.

"No, he thought. It must be my imagination.

"He went to bed and lay down. But still he could hear it.

"He opened the window to look, but the night was as dark as the inside

of a box. He couldn't see anything, so he went out to the back yard.

"He shone his torch behind the chicken house, frightening the rooster who gave a loud crow..."

"Cocker doodle-doo!" Shayla yelled, grabbing her cousin's shoulder.

"Shush," Michael said, in a shaky voice.

"He searched everywhere," Granny continued. "There was nothing. But, as he went back to the house, it came again. A whimper.

"Uncle William shone his torch

towards the road. And there it was."

"What?" the children spoke

together.

Shadows fluttered across Granny's face. "A baby, just sitting there. It was wearing a wide, cone-shaped hat so Uncle couldn't see its face. And then he noticed the feet, which were turned inwards.

"Uncle started to shake. Now he knew what it was – a douenne – a restless ghost child looking for a playmate. Old people often told tales about them. Mothers were warned that if a douenne calls your child's name they may be lost for ever.

" 'Why are you here?' Uncle asked. 'I'm lost,' said the douenne in a baby-like voice. 'Please take me back to the woods.'

"Uncle was terrified. But if he ignored the douenne, it might lure a sleepy child into danger.

" 'Carry me,' the douenne ordered.

"Uncle lifted the strange baby and headed towards the woods. And as Uncle walked, the douenne became heavier and heavier, until it felt like he was carrying a fully grown man."

"Ghosts shouldn't weigh anything," Michael said.

"Douennes do. At last, Uncle staggered to a stop by the woods. The douenne turned towards him. Uncle saw no eyes, no nose. No mouth.

"In a voice deeper than Uncle William's own, the douenne said, 'You can leave me here.'

"Then Uncle dropped the douenne and ran home as fast as he could!"

The children and their mothers clapped.

"Go on, Michael," Aunty Jess said.

"Tell us a good London ghost story!"

Michael looked thoughtful. "OK. But I need to get a snack first."

He returned with a paper bag.

"Ready?" He dipped his hand in and pulled out a tamarind ball.

Shayla waited for him to share.

He didn't.

"The graveyard near my school is more than 300 years old. It is Halloween. Du Shayne dares us to play a game of hide-and-seek there.

"We climb over the locked gates. It gets dark early in winter and the graveyard's full of mist and lots of old statues and tombs covered in ivy.

"I'm first to do the seeking. I count to 100 while everyone runs off."

Munch went another tamarind ball.

Was Michael eating them all? Shayla wondered.

"I open my eyes. There's Du Shayne, crouched beside a crooked headstone. He has his back to me.

So I creep up behind him and yell 'boo!'."

Michael passed the snack bag to Shayla. Happily, she put her hand inside as she listened to her cousin.

"Du Shayne stands up and turns towards me. He pushes back his hood. His face is a skull and his bony fingers reach out."

Shayla couldn't feel any tamarind balls. But what was this? Something round, and wet, and slimy...

"He drops something into my hand."

Shayla squeezed the objects.

"It's..."

Squeeze.

"His eyeballs!"

"Aaaagghhhhhh!" Shayla threw

the wet, squidgy thing onto the floor.

Click! The lights came back on.

Shayla looked down. Peeled

chennets! Sticky, juicy peeled chennets.

Mommy wiped away tears of

laughter. Even Granny was smiling.

"Well done, Michael," she said. "You

tell stories like a real Trinidadian."

Michael grinned back

triumphantly. "Thank you, Granny!"

Chapter Five

It was Saturday morning. Shayla was helping Mommy fold sheets. A deep, trumpeting noise came from outside. Shayla ran out and spotted Michael high in the branches of the lime tree with Granny's conch shell to his lips.

After a quick check for scary caterpillars, she climbed up to join him.

They sat side by side on the branch, watching the world below.

"What's it like, living in London?" Shayla said. "You seem to think it's much better than Arouca."

"London's brilliant. You're never bored. You can go on boat trips on the river. And there's this massive wheel that's taller than a building and you sit in a pod and look across the whole of the city. There's a zoo –"

"Trinidad's got a zoo."

"London's is bigger. And in winter

you can go ice-skating outside."

"You can't do that in Trinidad," Shayla said. "But we *do* have the beach. Mommy's going to take us there and we're leaving in an hour!"

The beach was a long drive away. The car wound its way along steep roads where waterfalls trickled down the hillside. Weaver-bird nests hung like old socks from high branches.

Then, at last...

Clear sky. The wrinkly sea. And fun.

The cousins sat at the water's edge. Waves splashed over them. Black cormorants swooped down for fish.

Later, they rummaged around in a river pool. Michael collected tiny black tadpoles.

"Frogpoles!" They hopped up his arm. "Not quite tadpoles or frogs."

Shayla showed him holes in the sand dunes where crabs lived. She told him about the turtles coming out at night to lay their eggs. You had to be very quiet if you wanted to see them.

Just before they went home, Mommy bought them snow cones – flaky ice and red syrup.

"So do you still think London is better than Trinidad?" Shayla asked her cousin as they got back in the car.

"Trinidad does have *some* cool things," Michael admitted.

The following day, Michael went off to play cricket with his cousins. Shayla decided to get to know the "pet" that Michael had brought from England. She climbed up to her favourite branch in the lime tree. Granny was throwing corn to the chickens below.

Shayla peered at the screen and fiddled with the buttons. Sometimes, the pet bleeped. Sometimes, the

pictures moved around a bit. But it didn't seem nearly as interesting to her as watching the marching ants or lazy iguanas.

She shook the pet hard to see what happened. Oops! It slipped out of her hands and tumbled down through the branches. The pet bounced off Granny's head and onto the floor.

Shayla clambered down.

"Sorry, Granny. I don't understand why girls in London like these things. Maybe I'm just not clever enough.

Do you think it would be different if I lived in London?"

Granny picked up the dusty toy and handed it to Shayla.

"You're fine just the way you are. If you lived in London, I would hardly ever see you."

"I know, Granny." Shayla sniffed back tears. "But why is Michael better than me at everything? He's even more like a true Trinidadian."

"Oh, Shayla!" Granny gave her a hug. "I'm sure there are some things

that you can do better than Michael.

Why don't you have some ice cream

to help you think?"

The old bike was propped against

the freezer. Shayla moved it aside.

"Yes!" Shayla stared at the bike.

"Ice cream is very good for thinking."

On Sunday afternoon, Mommy took Michael and Aunty Jess to visit elderly Tante Eve on the other side of Arouca. They were gone for a few hours.

Shayla stayed behind to be with Granny. Now she was on the porch keeping watch again. She squinted into the distance.

"I think I can see them." Three figures, one slightly shorter, had appeared at the end of the road.

"Are you ready?"

"Ah ha." Granny didn't sound sure.

"Well," Shayla said. "It's time."

Shayla burst out of the gate and ran towards her family.

"What's the matter?" Mommy said. "Is something wrong with Granny?"

Shayla pointed towards the house. "Look!"

They couldn't *see* anything, but they could hear it. A faint *ting ting*, getting louder, coming towards them.

"I don't believe it," Mommy said.

"It can't be…" Aunty Jess said.

But it was.

There, wobbling down the road

towards them on Grandpa's rusty old

bicycle, was...

"Granny!" Michael's voice was full

of admiration. She juddered to a stop

in front of them. "Mum told me you couldn't ride that bike!"

Granny winked at Shayla. "I had an excellent teacher."

Aunty Jess held the bike so Granny could get off. "But I tried to teach you and you pedalled backwards!"

"And then you landed in a bush," Mommy added.

"My father tried, and your grandpa. And even Uncle William." Granny beamed. "But only Shayla has managed to succeed."

Michael looked from one smiling person to another. "Well done, Shayla. That's one challenge I don't think I *could* have won!"

"Yes," laughed Aunty Jess. "Us Londoners have no patience. We're just too hot-headed, eh, Michael?"

"And too hot-mouthed," Shalya giggled, remembering the pepper sauce.

Michael blushed. "Truce?" he offered.

"Truce," Shayla agreed. "And now let's try and have some fun."

About the Author

Patrice Lawrence is Sussex-born, Hackney-living, from a Caribbean and Italian family. Patrice has always written – poetry until her teens, short stories in her twenties, screenplays in her thirties, and now a mash up of all of it. Her secret ambition is to write a horror story.

Other Stories From Different Cultures...

Bamba Beach

Pratima Mitchell

Times are hard for Hari's family – there are no fish left in the bay and they need a boat with an outboard motor to catch the ones further out. But that requires capital, and to get capital, they need to sell fish… The situation looks hopeless but Hari doesn't give up and soon help arrives from the most unlikely of places.

Bamba Beach is a contemporary story set in modern-day India.

ISBN: 978 1 4081 0895 6 £4.99

Other Stories From Different Cultures...

Andrew Fusek Peters

When Eva's uncle refuses to give her the cow he promised, her father takes him to court. The judge decides that whoever can answer his questions correctly will keep the cow. Eva does and wins the cow. She also wins the hand of the judge. But he soon discovers that there's more to having a clever wife than he bargained for.

Ever Clever Eva is a modern retelling of a traditional Czech tale.

ISBN: 978 0 7136 8883 2   £4.99

Year 5

Myths, Legends and Traditional Stories

The Path of Finn McCool • Sally Prue

The Barber's Clever Wife • Narinder Dhami

Taliesin • Maggie Pearson

Playscripts

Fool's Gold • David Calcutt

Time Switch • Steve Barlow and Steve Skidmore

Let's Go to London! • Kaye Umansky

Stories From Different Cultures

Granny Ting Ting • Patrice Lawrence

Ever Clever Eva • Andrew Fusek Peters

Bamba Beach • Pratima Mitchell